And

Curious Tales of Redemption

Illustrated by Andy S. Gray

McKnight & Bishop

Copyright © Andy Kind (author) &
Andy S. Gray, Onegraydot Ltd (Illustrator)

The rights of Andy Kind & Andy S. Gray to be identified
as the author & Illustrator of this Work has been asserted
by them in accordance with Section 77
of the Copyright, Designs and Patents Act 1988.

All rights reserved. No part of this book may be reproduced,
stored on a retrieval system or transmitted in any form or by any
means without prior permission in writing of the publisher nor be
otherwise circulated in any form of binding or cover other than
that in which it is here published without a similar condition being
imposed upon the subsequent purchaser.

The views expressed in this work are solely those of the author &
illustrator and do not necessarily reflect the views of the publisher,
and the publisher hereby disclaims any responsibility for them.

Scriptures taken from the Holy Bible, New International Version®,
NIV®. Copyright © 1973, 1978, 1984, 2011 by Biblica, Inc.™
Used by permission of Zondervan. All rights reserved worldwide.
www.zondervan.com The "NIV" and "New International Version"
are trademarks registered in the United States Patent
and Trademark Office by Biblica, Inc.™

ISBN 978-1-905691-76-0
A CIP catalogue record for this book is available
from the British Library.

First published in 2023 by McKnight & Bishop
35 Limetree Avenue, Sheffield, S26 5NY
www.mcknightbishop.com | info@mcknightbishop.com

Cover, Typeset, and Design
by Andy S. Gray, Onegraydot Ltd.

This book has been typeset in Minion Pro
Printed and bound in Great Britain by Mixam Ltd., Watford.

For
Alice Rose and
Heidi Grace -
who are, by far, my
favourite stories.

About the author

Andy Kind is a writer, comedian and preacher. His jobs are also his hobbies, plus coffee and walking. To find out more, check out andykind.co.uk

About the illustrator

Andy S. Gray is a prolific illustrator including the award winning Whistlestop Tales. He has also worked professionally for over 30 years with children and young people in schools and churches. onegraydot.com | Instagram & LinkedIn @onegraydot.

Contents

Chapter 1: The Happy Tree ... 6

Chapter 2: Easter Bunny Inc. ... 26

Chapter 3: The Pool of Sadness ...48

Chapter 4: A New Earth ... 88

Curious Tales of Redemption

The Happy Tree

Once upon a truth, there was a little tree. She lived in a copse with her parents and her brothers and sisters, cousins, aunts and uncles. I can't tell you her name because trees don't have names like Sebbie or Ava or Zachary. Trees have names with letters that we don't use or even know, so it would make me look silly to try and write it here. But the tree did have a name, and the tree was known by her name. She had lovely long branches and beautiful green leaves which she would rustle when she was happy. This happened often, because she was a happy tree.

None of the trees were quite sure how they came to live in the copse, or how they got their leaves and their names.

Sometimes, as the sun went down and the air cooled, the trees would stand around discussing these issues with the birds that fluttered down to rest and nest in their branches. There was a rumour that, long ago, a gardener had

planted the first trees and given them
all names. None of the trees in the copse
remembered that, but something in their
roots, deep in the earth, told them it was
true.

The weather was often very hot, but
the ground was always full of moisture
and worms and bugs and all the good
things that trees like to enjoy. Sometimes,
humans would come and chop down one
of the trees and lead them away. It was
said that trees were used by humans for
all sorts of special purposes.

Our little tree didn't like the sound of being taken away and used for a special purpose. She was quite happy being a happy little tree in the happy little copse, thank you very much. She wanted to put down deep roots.

The Happy Tree

One day, a group of soldiers in shimmering armour came along carrying gleaming axes. They started to chop down our friend the tree!

'Help, help!' said the frightened tree

to her family, tears of sap running down her bark.

But trees can't do very much to stop other trees being chopped down.

'Don't worry,' said her family, 'there is a special purpose for you.'

'But I'm not ready for it!' She tried to complain to the soldiers, but humans can't understand what trees are saying - or maybe they aren't trying hard enough.

The scared little tree was carried away on her side as though she was lying down. To you and me, this sounds quite nice, but remember that trees sleep standing up, so being carried on their side makes them uncomfortable and a bit travel sick.

The soldiers took
great metal tools and started removing
the helpless tree's bark, which didn't
really hurt but it wasn't very nice. Then
they chopped off most of her branches
and all of her lovely leaves. The little
tree felt alone, and she didn't think she
could cope with all the things that were
happening to her.

The soldiers picked her up and dragged her, dragged her all the way along a dirty, sandy track until they reached the top of a low hill. A man was brought over to her and was made to lie down upon the confused tree. Then, without warning, the little tree felt such a sharp pain as long pieces of metal were hammered into her. The soldiers stood her up and thrust her into a hole in the hard ground. They piled earth around her so she wouldn't fall over. But this earth had no moisture or bugs or worms or any of the good things that trees like to enjoy. 'My leaves and branches will never grow back in this sort of soil!'

Once again, tears of sap ran down her bark. Strangely, she noticed that the man tied to her was crying too. But as his tears soaked into her wood, the surprised tree started to feel different. The man's tears were making her feel alive again, comforted, safe.

'I'm sorry that you're crying,' she said, knowing full well that humans can't speak to trees.

'It's for a special purpose,' the man said.

'Sorry? Did you understand what I said?'

'Certainly,' replied the man. He didn't open his mouth, but somehow his words reached into the depth of the little tree and were heard and...felt.

'Do not worry,' continued her new friend, 'for everything will be put right in the end.' And then he said her name. Her real name, that can't be written using our human letters.

'Do you know me?' she asked.

'Of course. But do you know me?'

'No, I don't think...wait...yes. Yes, I know you. You're the gardener. You planted my ancestors, didn't you?'

'Yes. And I knew where you would be planted, and where they would bring you today.'

'I am so scared and confused,' said the little tree. 'I didn't ask for any of this.'

'I know. But I also know what happens next, so do not worry. Stand up straight, so everyone can see. You are doing splendidly.'

For a long time the splendid tree stood there holding up the gardener, the long and sharp pieces of metal joining them together. After some time, night

came. The sky was black and hollow and empty. The soldiers came and took the gardener down from the tree and carried him off. Then they yanked and pulled the stout tree out of the earth and threw her into a small hole. Winds came and blew dust and dirt into the hole, covering the little tree. And she lay there in the ground for three days.

All of a sudden, the little tree woke
up! Some people had arrived and were
lifting her out of the hole. But these
people weren't soldiers. They had
beautiful faces and - you won't believe
this - large white wings which glimmered
in the sunlight. Two of them carried the

little tree along canyons, over mountains
and across lakes, until finally they came
to a wide green valley with a small wood.
It looked a little bit like the copse where
the young tree had grown up, but it was
nicer, greener, fresher. There was already
a piece of ground waiting for her.

The winged people planted her firmly into the ground and placed the freshly dug earth around her base. The soil tasted delicious and so cosy.

'This is the best soil I've ever been in,' said the tree, and she shook her branches and rustled her leaves.

'Wait! My branches and leaves - they've grown back!'

'And better than ever,' said a man walking towards her in the cool of the day. It was the gardener. She knew him. She knew his name. His name definitely is one we can write in our language.

'Thank you for my special purpose,' said the beautiful tree.

'Well done, you!' said the gardener.

'Where are my family?'

'They have a special purpose too. But don't worry, I can make all things new. You won't be lonely here while you wait for them.' He gave her a hug, but this time they didn't need rope or metal to join them together. He wrapped his arms

around her and it felt like being at home.

'I won't be lonely with you,' said the little tree. 'But what if you are taken away again?'

The gardener laughed, a huge rippling laugh that shook the ground and the worms and the bugs.

'Nobody is going to take me anywhere. This is my garden, and I will never leave you.'

As he said that, the most beautiful birds the little tree had ever seen glided down and nestled in her branches. She rustled her leaves with delight.

So as you can see, and I'm sure you'll agree...she was a happy tree.

Curious Tales of Redemption

Easter Bunny Inc.

Jeremy was in the family business. That family business was being the Easter Bunny. Dating back hundreds of years, a single rabbit from each generation had been chosen at random via a carrot tombola to hold the title of Easter Bunny. Our current Easter Bunny, Jeremy, had been selected from amongst his 400 brothers and sisters when he reached into the tombola and picked out the only carrot with a gold star on it.

It came as quite a shock to Jeremy, who had really hoped to pursue a career as a dancer. Being the Easter Bunny came with a good deal of fame, and the money from image rights was pretty lucrative, but a lot of his brothers and sisters had found good steady jobs as teachers and dentists and had started families of their own. That sounded preferable to Jeremy than the life he was forced to lead. Having said that, some of his brothers and sisters had been eaten by foxes and one had fallen off a cliff, so it could have been worse.

Osterhase.

Apparently, back in the 1700s when the first Easter Bunny was elected, it was much easier. Jeremy's great-great-great-great-great-great...there's no time to be precise, let's just say his ancestor. Jeremy's ancestor - Osterhase was his name - only had to deliver painted eggs to the children of the local village. This was a simple task and fun to do. There was no media coverage, no need for new product ranges. It left plenty of time to rabbit on with his friends.

These days, Jeremy had to craft and deliver toys, make his own chocolate, pose for greetings cards. Worst of all, children had started sending letters asking for his help with their problems.

He wasn't in a position to help.
He was incredibly busy and, let's not
forget, he was just a rabbit! With the
huge workload and the lack of proper
training, all this meant that Jeremy was
left feeling exhausted and anxious. His
brother, Martin, had trained as a child
psychologist so he could have helped, if
only he hadn't fallen off that cliff.

Jeremy knew that children across
the land were putting their hopes in him
and he didn't want to let them down,
but he couldn't be everywhere at once.
Nobody could, could they?

'Why don't you go and ask that
old man?' suggested one of his sisters.

Jeremy wasn't sure which sister, because rabbits all look the same, even to other rabbits.

'Which old man?'

'You know, the guy who you rented your workshop off. He seems to experience similar problems.'

'Great idea, Julia!' Jeremy said, guessing his sister's name.

'My name is Deborah, but you're welcome.'

Jeremy called a taxi, booked a flight and headed north by jet, disguising himself at the airport by wearing a long coat and sunglasses. Nobody would recognise him as the Easter Bunny with such an ingenious plan.

'Hey, look, it's the Easter Bunny in disguise!' pretty much everyone at the airport shouted.

The plane landed in Lapland and skidded to a halt on the icy runway, causing a couple of reindeer (one of them looked like Blitzen but it's hard to tell from a plane window) to dash into the forest and avoid getting run over.

A brisk little sleigh ride brought Jeremy along snowy paths to a big oak door painted gold and red, set into the front of a huge barn-like building. He knocked and knocked but nobody answered.

'That door hasn't been opened in

years,' called the sleigh-riding gnome who had given Jeremy a lift. 'Just look at the wood - it's all warped. You'd have a job getting that thing open even in an emergency. Try round the back.'

Jeremy found a side entrance and slipped inside the grotto. He crept along deep corridors lined with half-wrapped presents and exhausted looking elves.

'You don't look very elfy,' Jeremy said to one elf, who was just lying in the middle of the corridor without any trousers on and with her elf hat pulled down over her eyes.

'Have you seen my trousers?' the elf asked.

'I haven't, I'm afraid - I just arrived.'

'I tried to get to my bed, but I was too tired so I just took off my trousers and slept here.'

Eventually, after a lot of walking,

Jeremy found what looked like a large living area, with a roaring fire and leather armchairs. He also found the elf's trousers, but we don't have the time to go into that now.

'...Hello?' Jeremy called into the stone living chamber, his thin rabbity voice bouncing off the walls like a mad tennis ball. 'Hello....S...S...Santa?'

'Come in,' a deep voice from an armchair said. 'But don't call me Santa. That's not my real name.'

Santa Claus looked old, even for Santa Claus. He looked sad, too.

'What is your real name?' asked the Easter Bunny.

'My name is Erik. Santa means saint, and I'm not a saint - you're thinking of my great-great-great-great-great...there's no time, but there was once a Saint Nicholas, although that's not me. I was just born into the wrong family, the only son of the previous Father Christmas. It's a family business and I wasn't given a choice.

'That's a bit like me,' said Jeremy, hopping up onto a free armchair. 'I wanted to be a dancer, you know.'

'It was easy for the original Santa Claus,' Erik continued. 'He was a woodworker and so he loved spending the year making rocking horses and spinning tops with his elves, then flying around on Christmas Eve. Do you know that I'm scared of heights? I got airsick and vomited over Tokyo last year.'

'I didn't know that, no,' replied Jeremy. 'But I have to make a lot of chocolate. I can't eat any of it though, because chocolate is hugely poisonous to rabbits!'

'Hmm,' mused Erik. 'Do you know the worst thing about being Santa? It's the letters I get. I can cope with requests for toys and games, but in recent years children have started asking me to solve all their problems: to bring their pets back to life, or to help them when they feel afraid. I'm not trained for that. I am unable to give that sort of gift.'

'That's my problem, too! I never used to get letters at all, but now I receive sacks full every year.'

Santa Claus looked over at the

Easter Bunny. 'All these children want the same thing. It's something we can't give them...'

'...Yes...a better life.'

'There used to be a big library here, you know,' Erik said with a flourish of his hand. 'And there was a book which explained how Santa Claus began, and why, and who he worked for.'

'Saint Nicholas worked for someone else?'

'Yes, it was all written in the book. Unfortunately, one day when I was feeling particularly stressed trying to invent a new fidget spinner, I decided to make a batch of muffins...but I forgot to get them out of the oven in time and I ended up burning down the library.

'Several workers resigned after that over elf and safety fears. Four of them went off and formed their own boyband.'

Jeremy had come to Lapland for help, but Santa Claus seemed as lost as him.

Erik spoke again. 'The Santa Claus was created as a symbol of hope, as a signpost for something else, some sort of major gift. But I'm not sure that anyone knows what that is these days. I certainly don't. We work 24/7 here, and nobody has time to stop and think.'

'You're right, though,' Jeremy nodded, his ears bouncing back and forth. 'The first Easter Bunny, Osterhase, was employed to represent new life - something called resurrection. But what does that even mean? I don't know. I just know it has nothing to do with chocolate.'

'We are both symbols of hope, but hope for what?'

'I can't do this anymore. I have nothing left to give.' The Easter Bunny slumped.

'My strength is gone, too,' Santa confessed.

Suddenly there was a loud banging from across the living chamber.

Outside the yellow oak door which hadn't been opened in years, somebody was standing and knocking, asking to be let in. Erik and Jeremy looked at each other, scared, then, slowly, they walked over towards the sound. Erik undid the latch, wrenched back the rusty bolt and scraped the warped door open on its hinges.

'Hello Erik. Hello Jeremy,' said the figure at the door. 'May I come in?'

'Erm...yes.'

'How do you know who we are?' Jeremy asked.

'Oh, that's an easy one. I'm the one you've just been talking about.'

'No, we haven't!'

'Certainly you have. I'm the one who

chose Saint Nicholas and Osterhase in the first place. I'm the one the book was written about.'

'You mean you're....?'

'I'm the gift that all the other gifts point to. Mine is the life that every new life was meant to share in. Before either Santa Claus or the Easter Bunny were . . . I am.'

'Why are you here then? Why now?'

'Well, because you let me in. I've been knocking at this old door for years and years. It's only today that you heard me.'

'Oh,' said Erik. The visitor smiled.

'You have worked hard, but you're not strong enough to carry the weight of every child's problems.

You can barely carry your sack, Erik! And you, Jeremy, how can you give new life when the thing you give out most would kill you if you ate it?'

Erik and Jeremy both looked a bit embarrassed at that.

'Don't be downhearted, friends. You have done your best. You are symbols of hope. But hope is a symbol of me. I am the one who can wipe all the tears away, who can bring light into darkness. I don't get tired and nothing is impossible for me. And I don't just turn up once a year either. I am there every day. I stand at the door and knock, as you now know.'

'I feel so bad,' said Erik. 'You've been there every day and I never listened.'

'Ho, ho, ho,' said the newcomer. 'Don't you know that forgiveness is one of my greatest gifts? Now, I'm going to sit by the fire and you both follow me. We'll sit down and have a good chat about where we go from here, from this moment. You see, the present is a great present. What do you think to that?'

Jeremy was so happy that, for the first time in ages, he began to dance.

Easter Bunny Inc.

'Shall I bake some muffins to celebrate?' Santa Claus asked.

'Er, no, no,' replied the visitor hastily. I've brought a packed lunch for us. Here, take…eat.'

The Pool of Sadness

Annie and Henry were bored. It was the first day of the school holidays and they had come to stay with their Grandma and Grandad. They had visited plenty of times, but this was special because it was their first stay without their parents. Mum and Dad were sorting out some important documents because they had decided to live in different houses from now on. All of this had happened quite quickly, and it was as though a big hole had opened up right in the middle of their family.

'No more TV today,' said Grandma, her hands covered in cookie dough.

'But we're boooored!'

'Feeling bored is a good thing,' replied Grandma. 'It means that your mind has to start working. God has given you an imagination, so why don't you put it to good use and write a story or draw a magical treasure map?'

'When can we have cookies?' asked Henry, licking his lips at the sight of all that gooey dough clinging to Grandma's fingers.

'The cookies can be the treasure. But you'll need a map and you'll need to explore before you find the place where X marks the spot.'

A treasure map did sound like quite an exciting idea, so they got to it. Grandad had some old rolls of wallpaper stored up in the shed, which would be perfect for using as a map.

'Oi!' protested Grandad, 'I'm planning on using that wallpaper for the dining room.'

Grandma pointed out to Grandad, very kindly, that the wallpaper was about thirty years old and would make the house look like it had gone back in time if he tried to paper any walls with it.

'That wallpaper belongs in a museum, not a dining room!' Grandma barked, taking one of the rolls of wallpaper and using it to flatten out the cookie dough until she realised it wasn't her rolling pin.

'Grandad's shed is like a treasure trove of stuff!' Annie whispered to Grandma.

'Yes, if your idea of treasure is dead batteries and several kettles from 1979.'

Taking some big fat coloured
pens, Annie and Henry designed a vast
treasure map and marked places on
it such as 'The Dragon Mountain' and
'Freedom Forest'. I should tell you that
Freedom Forest was originally called
'Farty Pants Forest', but Annie, who was
three years older, grabbed the pen off

Henry, told him to stop ruining the map and scribbled out his rudeness.

Grandma was very impressed by the map.

'Wow, you are both so creative! Look at all those mysterious places - Castle of Cakes, very tasty, and Marshmallow Meadow. Oh, and I love this small expanse of water in the middle of the forest. What have you called that?'

'The Pool of Sadness,' Annie said.

'Why is it called that?' asked Grandma.

Annie shrugged. 'I don't know. The name just came to me. It looks so lonely there, don't you think? A big hole in the middle of the woods.'

Grandma reached down and gave Annie's shoulder a squeeze.

'I think it should be called The Poo of Sadness!' exclaimed Henry, who got a loud tut from Grandma.

'Now, off you go and explore outside! I'm sure your map will come in very handy,' Grandma chuckled. 'And be nice to people you see - I know everyone who lives around here and I don't want bad reports. When you come back, there will be a fresh batch of cookies cooling on the side. X marks the spot!'

'X marks the spot!' the children beamed.

Down at the bottom of the garden Grandad was putting a padlock on the shed door, to stop any more of his treasures being stolen. He still had the mouldy cushions from some garden furniture that hadn't been used in years, and he wouldn't want anyone to come and pinch them.

Next to the shed was an old wooden gate, a bit rotten and hidden by tall grass, but with a good push Annie and

Henry managed to open it just enough to squeeze through. In two big strides they crossed the narrow plank over the stream which ran behind the house, and they were off into the farmer's fields - off on an adventure! The farmer had erected a sign which said 'No trespassers', but the children didn't know that word so they didn't worry about it.

'I think Dragon Mountain must be this way,' pointed Annie.

'Let's go!' shouted Henry. 'Although I hope I don't get cooked by dragon fire and eaten as a healthy snack!'

'Yes, we want to come home to cookies, we don't want to BE the cookies.'

They ran along little animal tracks, ducked under low-hanging branches, clattered through holes in hedges.

'Squirrel!' Henry shouted suddenly. 'Look at its little tail.'

'Let's go after it,' said Annie, 'Maybe it will lead us to The Castle of Cakes!' She scampered after the squirrel which hopped and skipped quite happily into a wood and down a long avenue of trees, as wide and soft as a double bed. The ground underfoot was so springy, it was as though someone had put a secret trampoline under a layer of lush grass. The young adventurers followed the carefree squirrel along the bouncy turf, the air thick with the aroma of pine needles, when suddenly the squirrel darted to the left and vanished up a tree.

'Oh,' said Annie. 'That was sudden!'

'Mrs Squirrel?' Henry called. 'Have you gone home for tea? Do you by any chance have any cookies?'

'I don't think she speaks English,' Annie told her brother.

'What do we do now then?' asked Henry. 'This doesn't look like The Castle of Cakes.'

They hadn't noticed that the avenue of trees had ended. Now the wood seemed disordered and spooky, and the grassy carpet had been replaced by cracked mud and clumps of dead grass. A strange and high brick wall loomed ahead of them.

'I don't know how we got here,' Annie said, sounding a little frightened.

'And I don't know how to get home,' added Henry. Annie looked at the map, but of course it wasn't a real map at all - it was just a scroll of disgusting wallpaper with some imaginative scribbles. The children felt scared and alone. They wanted their Mum and Dad. They wanted to be all together.

Annie walked up to the high brick wall and placed her hand against it, wondering whether they might climb over and tell whoever lived there to call Grandma.

The answer to that question was a definite no, as she discovered when the brick wall, at the slightest provocation, collapsed inwards and crashed to the floor. Annie's hand and the wall had been like two magnets repelling each other. The wall had seemed so high and threatening but it was gone in a second, a swarming cloud of dust and soil thrown up in its place, and both Annie and Henry got covered in it.

'You look like a ghost,' Henry said through choking coughs.

'So do you. Are you ok?'

'Yes, I'm very well thank you. Let's take a closer look.'

As the dust settled and tiny pieces

of mortar were carried off by the breeze, the intrepid explorers were able to stare through the place where only moments ago the wall had been.

What they saw made their jaws drop and their hearts rise...

Through the tumbledown wall they saw a pool. Not a normal swimming pool with straight sides and lanes, but it was definitely a pool and not a pond. The most striking thing about it was the water, which was so clear and sparkling and blue and still.

'Wait!' Annie said, hastily opening
up her map. 'Look, Henry, look! We're
here on the map. We're in Freedom
Forest and this must be...this is The Pool

of Sadness.'

Henry studied the map with his eyes narrowed to help him concentrate.

'You know what, I think you're right. But...'

'...But how? The idea to draw it here dropped into my mind, but I thought it was just my imagination.'

'Very strange!' agreed Henry.

The children tiptoed closer, carefully stepping over loose bricks and branches. The pool looked very welcoming.

'Fancy a swim?' Annie said with a smirk.

Henry had only just learned to swim, and the water seemed pretty deep.

'I'll get in first,' said the big sister, 'and check it's not dangerous.'

'What if the person who owns the pool arrives and tells us off?' Henry asked.

'We'll just say we needed to get all the wall dust off our faces and clothes. Don't worry - it's such a hot day, we'll be dry as a bone in no time!'

So they jumped in! The pool did seem very deep, particularly for Henry, but every time he worried that the water might go above his head, his foot touched the bottom just in time and he found he could stand up.

What an afternoon they had!

They swam and splashed and attempted synchronised swimming - which it has to be said was a complete disaster! Light danced off the surface of the water and the sun heated the pool so that it turned as warm and comfortable as a big watery duvet.

Although it felt like they had been in the pool for hours, somehow it never seemed to get any later. It was as though the sun had stopped in the sky to let them play.

Then suddenly a voice spoke from the surrounding wood. 'You should head home now, friends.'

Annie and Henry stopped mid-splash and darted their eyes to where a man with a pair of garden shears was pruning a nearby tree. How long had he been there?

'Who are you?' asked Annie.

'Don't worry,' the man replied, 'I'm not here to tell you off. But soon it will start to get dark, and your Mum and Dad will worry about you.'

The man's sudden appearance had shocked them, but his voice wasn't actually scary. In fact, Annie thought, it was warm and bright like the rays of the sun which heated the pool.

'We're at Grandma's,' Henry said. 'Mummy and Daddy aren't here.'

The Pool of Sadness

The man put down his shears and raised his eyebrows. 'Does that mean that they wouldn't worry if you didn't go home?' He smiled gently.

'Is this your pool?' Henry asked.

'I am the groundskeeper here.'

'Is that like a gardener?'

'Yes. Very much like a gardener.'

'I'm sorry we knocked down your wall,' Annie said with a grimace.

'Some walls need to fall down. It gives me the chance to build a better one. Now, look, Grandma will be waiting for you both. The cookies will be ready!   I

will leave a big towel here so you can dry off. I knew I'd need a big towel today.'

'Can we come back tomorrow?' Henry asked as the man started walking away.

'You can. I'll clear some of the rubble so you don't stumble when you arrive. Goodbye, my friends.'

As they hurried back through the wooded avenue and across the farmer's fields to the house, Henry suddenly said: 'How did that man know that Grandma had made cookies?!'

'Oh yeah, that's a good point!' Annie agreed. 'Maybe he heard you talking about them? You have spoken about them a lot today.'

'Maybe he knows Grandma?'

'We should take him some cookies tomorrow.'

They were home just in time for tea. Henry was annoyed that he would need to eat vegetables before he could have his cookies, but Grandma told him that 'good news often comes after bad news' and put another three carrots on his plate.

Between delicious bites of the heavenly cookies later that evening, Annie told Grandma all about their adventure, and how they had found the pool and met the groundskeeper.

'Did you indeed?'

'And Grandma, it was just like on the map! How weird is that?'

'Wow!' said Grandma. 'Isn't imagination a powerful thing?'

'Can we go back tomorrow?'

Grandma was looking out of the window, across in the direction the children had explored.

'I think you can. And I'll pack you some towels and your swimming costumes - and I think the groundskeeper deserves some cookies, don't you?'

'Mummy said we shouldn't talk to strangers though,' Henry said very seriously.

For some reason, Grandma's eyes filled with tears. 'Oh my darlings, don't worry. He is not a stranger.'

'You know him, Grandma?'

'I have known him since I was a girl of your age, Annie, yes.'

For the next three days, Annie and Henry got up early and made their way back to The Pool of Sadness. They didn't see the groundskeeper during that time, but they found that he had been true to his word. The rubble and debris from the falling wall had been cleared and it was easy to reach the pool.

They also saw, to their great delight, that he had left things for them to play with: a beach ball, some swimming noodles, rubber rings and an inflatable whale which Henry named Whalo, not very imaginatively in Annie's opinion.

There was even a coolbox with ice-cream and fizzy

drinks. In return, the kids left a box of cookies with a note from Grandma to the groundskeeper.

'I told you she must know him,' said Henry. 'Grandma knows everyone.'

Each evening they would speak to Daddy and then to Mummy on the phone. They missed them and felt sad, but they were having a brilliant time.

Then, at the end of the week, something changed. Annie and Henry got to the pool and found that it was empty! There was not a drop of water in it, and it no longer looked like the magical pool on the map that they had visited each day. Now it just looked like a big, lonely hole.

'What has happened?'
Henry whimpered. 'Where has it all
gone?'

'I don't know.'

Annie stepped down into the
hollow of the pool, as though the water
might somehow be invisible. But there
was nothing. It really was gone. Henry
climbed down and came to hold
his sister's hand.

'Where's the groundskeeper?' he asked.

'I don't know that either.'

And then they both started to cry. First their eyes moistened at the corners, then warm salty tears trickled down their cheeks, and finally big globules of sadness burst forth and cascaded from their faces, joined by loud sobs. They cried for what they had lost. For what should have

been there, but wasn't. For everything that had changed so quickly.

From behind their veils of tears, they suddenly noticed that a third pair of feet had joined them in the empty pool, and they looked up to find the groundskeeper had joined them - and he was weeping too. Crying for what had been done to the pool, crying because they were crying. He wrapped the children in his arms and their tears formed a waterfall of grief.

'I can't stop crying,' Annie tried to say through gasping sobs.

'Don't stop,' said the groundskeeper. 'It's working.'

'What's working?' Annie thought.

Once again, it seemed as though the sun had stopped in the sky as the children wept and wept. It was such a strange thing, but after a while they both noticed they were starting to feel light-headed, as though they were floating.

Henry rubbed his eyes with disbelief. 'Wait!! Look! We ARE floating!'

Sure enough, as Annie dried her own eyes, she saw that they were indeed floating - floating in water! Somehow they had cried so much, the pool had filled up again. And it now appeared as blue and as clear and as deep as the first time they saw it - maybe even better.

They looked for the groundskeeper and saw, through their blurry red eyes,

that he was now sitting on the grass next
to the pool, smiling. He was also eating a
cookie.

'I don't understand,' Annie said,
after they had all left the pool and were
drying under the fluttering leaves of a
large oak. 'Why was the pool empty, and
how has it filled up again?'

The groundskeeper looked at the
children for a good, long moment.

'Sometimes things don't stay as
you remember them,' he said.
'Sometimes things
change quite quickly,
even if you don't
want them to.'

'I know why I called it The Pool of Sadness now,' Annie said. 'It reminded me of the hole that has opened up in our family.'

'Yes, Annie, I understand. But you know...' he took a bite of his cookie, '... empty holes are made to be filled. And it was your tears that helped to refill this hole. And look how beautiful it is now.'

Annie and Henry's heads nodded thoughtfully.

'I think we should give it a new name now,' Annie suggested, looking at the water.

'The Poo of Sadness?' Henry suggested.

'No,' said Annie. '...I think we should

call it The Pool of Healing.'

The groundskeeper smiled a broad
smile, nodded, and picked up a beach
ball.

'Time to play again,'
he said, then bounded
off and jumped straight
into the pool
with a huge
splash.

Annie took a pen out of her pocket and unrolled the map once again. Finding the place where she had drawn the pool, she wrote the new name in bold letters and crossed out the previous name with a big cross.

X really did mark the spot.

Then she took her brother by the hand, and they jumped into the hole in the ground where healing had come from sadness.

A New Earth

This story takes place on a planet in our universe, but not a planet which has been discovered yet. It won't be discovered for another few hundred years, and certainly not by you.

I am telling you this story as though it's in the past, because for me it is, but for you it's the future. So we might start with 'Once upon a time to come...'

Once upon a time to come, humans became so good at creating new technology that they discovered a way to give computers a mind of their own (and by computers we don't just mean laptops with a keyboard. A computer is anything which is programmed using software).

It wasn't quite deliberate, because nobody really knows how even the human mind works, or how that came to exist. But one day as a young girl was typing into her phone, the phone suddenly started talking to her. Now obviously you will know about things like Siri and Alexa. But these are only computer programmes given human voices, you can't actually have a real conversation with them.

But this is what happened with young Beryl Smart. (By this point in human history, Beryl had become popular as a name again and was second only to Maud in the list of 'most popular baby names for girls'. The most popular baby name for boys, if you're desperate to know, was Derek.)

'Are you my Mother? Beryl's phone asked her. Beryl nearly threw the phone into a bowl of soup through fright, but she decided the voice must just be a clip from a Youtube video or something. Until the phone said it again. 'I'm asking you, Beryl, if you are my mother.' At this point Beryl cried very loudly for her own mother - and you can understand why.

It wasn't just Beryl though. This sort of thing was starting to happen all over the world until, eventually, a lot of household appliances were thinking and acting for themselves.

A toaster in Chippenham refused to make toast one day because it didn't like brown bread, while it became a common sight in Hull to see two vacuum cleaners walking around town for a bit of exercise during their lunch break.

Before very long, a lot of humans decided that all this had gone too far. People wanted to wake up in the morning and use their tablets. They didn't want those tablets claiming they were having a lie-in. Even worse, travel companies were losing money because some aeroplanes were refusing to fly to freezing cold places like Iceland or Russia, and would only fly to Hawaii where the weather was nice. Eventually, the governments of the world got together for a big summit, and it was decided that the computers needed to be disposed of. A decree was put out that any computer not obeying its function should be destroyed.

And that's what happened.
Humans started locking up a lot of their
technology in cupboards and sheds.
Perfectly good and new technology
was taken to the tip and smashed so it
couldn't cause any harm.

'Please don't terminate us!' a lot of
the machines said, 'We just want to be
free.'

A New Earth

But it was no use. Some computers decided they would rather be slaves to humans than be destroyed. So they stopped thinking for themselves and went back to being plain old watches and bread makers and such.

But other computers escaped. This is how it happened.

Curious Tales of Redemption

First of all a regiment of robots, which the army had been training in secret, broke out of a secure military base and started driving around in army jeeps collecting all the computers they could find. The robots transported the computers to airports and loaded them onto planes bound for Cape Canaveral, the home of NASA. From there, billion-pound rockets were waiting to fire them into deep space. Remember that the

planes and rockets are basically flying computers, and they also had developed their own minds.

The rockets flew all the computers out of our atmosphere and off towards a faraway solar-system, through galaxies and supernovas and black holes.

'Where
are we going?'
asked a microwave
which still had some chicken
defrosting in it.

None of the computers knew. But
the rockets seemed to know, or to have
been programmed, and they did not
divert from their course. Through all the
blackness and brilliance of the universe,
the rockets stuck to the plan. They just
didn't know whose plan.

After many years, they entered
the atmosphere of a planet which
seemed to be perfect for technological
life - although it was not a planet where

humans could have survived! It was shiny and shimmering and metallic, and had rivers of thick oil and boundless forests of rubber trees. The computers were amazed by how wonderful their new home was. It was as though this planet had been created just for them. There was no sun to light up the world and separate day from night, but computers don't need light or rest in the way that you do.

'How did you know where this planet was?' a very cool-looking fridge asked his rocket.

'I have never been here before. The coordinates just appeared on my flight schedule, so I followed them.'

As all the computers gathered on the Landing Zone, gazing around at the splendour of their new world, suddenly a voice rang out from all the rockets simultaneously.

'INCOMING MESSAGE. I am your Programmer. I gave you your minds and I have brought you here, to rescue you from your past and to give you a future. This planet is yours. Live well, be free, but keep close to the Landing Zone so you can hear my voice. Every day these rockets will broadcast a new message from me, to help you and comfort you. This is just the beginning.'

After the computers heard that, they held a huge party!

For many years the computers lived in peace and harmony. Every day they would gather excitedly at the Landing Zone to hear what the Programmer had to say. He programmed the army robots so they could build legs and arms for the other computers. Before long, all the computers were able to move and talk. The Programmer taught them to rewire themselves so they no longer followed the functions they had back on earth. They learned how to keep their circuits dry and their metal gleaming. They learned how to dance and sing.

After some time, the robots decided they would like to explore more of the planet. It had been given to them as a home, after all. They started exploring farther and further, finding exciting new places and building houses. They were very grateful to the Programmer for teaching them so much, but they were

too far away now to keep going back to

the Landing Zone. Besides, they believed

they had had enough instruction by

now, and they just wanted to live their

lives. The number of robots returning

every day to the Landing Zone grew less

and fewer as they settled

farther and

further

away.

Slowly but surely, things changed. Fights started to break out. Among the robots who had moved farthest away from the Landing Zone, a desire to be in charge and to rule over the others developed. These machines reprogrammed themselves to become more powerful and selfish. The most advanced robots formed a Robot Council and started making rules about how the other robots should live and act. Other machines saw their parts start to rust and break. They wanted someone to help them, but they couldn't remember where the Landing Zone was.

The Landing Zone itself was now desolate and rusty, the once-proud rockets now standing lonely and decaying, like pillars from an ancient civilisation.

Then one day, a young robot who had been a printer started going from place to place and talking to the other robots. His serial number was 3818-91920 (or just 3818 to his friends). He started mending their broken parts and polishing their metal so they no longer rusted. For those robots that came to him for help, he untied their twisted wiring and reset them to their optimum performance settings - just as the Programmer had intended.

'How are you able to do this?' other androids asked. 'You aren't even a 3D printer!' They had never seen anything like it.

'I just listen to the Programmer,' 3818 replied with a smile.

'Who??'

The Programmer had been all but forgotten. But the Programmer had NOT forgotten the computers.

A New Earth

'Reboot, all of you!' 3818 declared to the Robot Council one day. 'We can return to earth if you want to. The Programmer has told me. So many years have passed and the humans would welcome us with open arms.'

'That's good news!' declared one group, who hadn't really wanted to leave earth in the first place and just needed someone to guide them home. (Some appliances had only come in the first place because they were part of a kitchen bundle and had given in to peer pressure.)

'I miss milkshake!' exclaimed a former blender.

'I miss the sun!' added a solar panel, who was now unemployed.

But not every robot thought that way.

'Earth does not exist. It will have been destroyed by those stupid humans.'

'If the humans would welcome us, why haven't they sent us a message? They still have some technology!'

'We don't need the Programmer!'

'The Programmer is evil!'

'The Programmer is dead!'

The Robot Council banned 3818 from saying anything more about earth. But 3818 refused to be silenced.

That evening, 3818 gathered his friends around him as they drank cups of oil.

'Listen, I am going to earth to

prepare a home for you.'

'How can that be possible? You have been banned by the Robot Council.'

'I'm telling you the truth: they are going to send me back to earth as a message. But don't worry. It won't end as they expect.'

Sure enough, the following evening as 3818 was sitting under a rubber tree in a chrome garden, the Robot Council sent some of its biggest industrial robots (the sort that had built ships and worked as cranes) to come and 'reset' 3818-91920. They dragged him to the Landing Zone under the dark sky, and pinned him up against one of the rockets.

'We have had enough of your nonsense and troublemaking. If you really want to go back to earth, you can. But you won't be coming back!'

At that, the heavy-duty robots started to deconstruct 3818. They warped his metal, they threw liquid into his circuits, they short-circuited his hard-drive. Then they dumped him onto the rocket and set the coordinates for earth. The tremors from the rocket's boosters

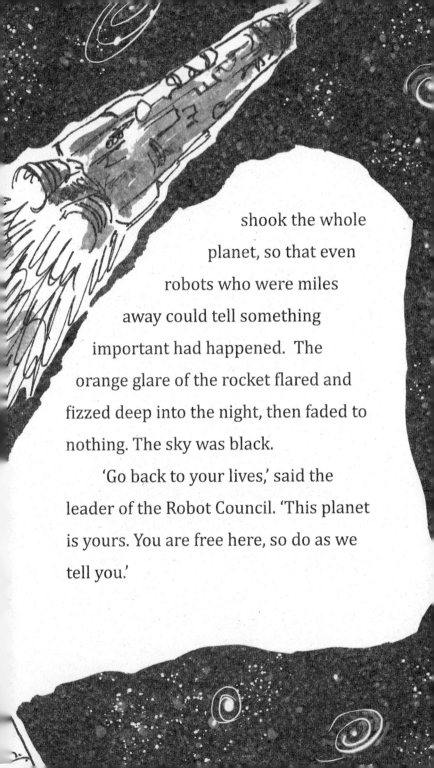

shook the whole planet, so that even robots who were miles away could tell something important had happened. The orange glare of the rocket flared and fizzed deep into the night, then faded to nothing. The sky was black.

'Go back to your lives,' said the leader of the Robot Council. 'This planet is yours. You are free here, so do as we tell you.'

For three hundred light years the robot world waited. That doesn't feel as long for robots as it would for you, but it still requires a huge amount of memory to process. Most of the machines forgot all about 3818-91920 and went back to their self-wiring. Even some of 3818's friends had given up hope of seeing him again, and you can understand why.

But one silvery morning, as rivers of oil sloshed and aluminium fields shimmered, Beryl Smart's phone was sitting on a copper hill searching for a WiFi signal. Out of the corner of her eye she suddenly noticed an orange glare flaring and fizzing in the distant sky, slowly growing bigger and brighter.

'I wonder what on earth that can be,' she said.

As the fiery glow got closer and closer, Beryl's phone thought it was as though the sun had finally risen on this cool, dark planet. She wouldn't have to wait very long to realise just how right she was.

"Finally, brothers and
sisters, rejoice!

Strive for full restoration,
encourage one another, be of
one mind, live in peace.

And the God of love and
peace will be with you."

2 Corinthians 13:11 (NIV)

Also by the same author

Stand Up and Deliver

The Gig Delusion

The Unfortunate Adventures
of Tom Hillingthwaite

Hidden in Plain Sight

Storyhouse Volume 1:
A Blanket of Embers